THIS BOOK
BELONGS TO

Victoria Schreiber

361 00425 7

MADE AND PRINTED IN GREAT BRITAIN BY PURNELL AND SONS, LTD.,
PAULTON (SOMERSET) AND LONDON

YOU FUNNY LITTLE NODDY!

BY
Enid Blyton

CONTENTS

LONDON
SAMPSON LOW, MARSTON & CO., LTD.
AND THE RICHARDS PRESS, LTD.

"IT DOESN'T MATTER IF IT'S TOO BIG, IT WILL KEEP YOU DRY,"
SAID BIG-EARS

6

IT'S RAINING

PITTER-PATTER, splish, splash, drip-drip-drip! Pitter-patter, splish-splash. . . .

Whatever was that noise? Noddy woke up with a jump. He sat up in bed, rubbing his eyes.

Pitter-patter, pitter-patter, drip-drip, splash, splish. . . .

"Goodness—it's RAINING!" said little Noddy. "I quite thought I must have left my tap dripping." He jumped out of bed and ran to the window. He could hardly see out of it because of the raindrops running down the pane.

Noddy sang a little song.

"I really love a rainy day,
With puddles in the street,
And raindrops bumping on my nose,
And splishy-splashy feet!
I wish I was a little duck
That didn't wear a mac,
I'd like to feel the raindrops run
All down my feathery back!
I really love a——"

A loud knock came at the door and made Noddy jump. "Milko!" said a voice, and the door opened. There stood the milkman, dripping wet from head to foot.

"I won't come in and tap your head

to make it nod this morning," said the milkman.
"I'm too wet. Noddy, hurry and dress yourself.
It's so wet this morning that there will be lots
of people who will want to hire your car!"

"Oooh, yes! I hadn't thought of that," said
little Noddy. "Here I am still in my pyjamas.
Do you like them, milkman?—they're new."

"Very nice," said the milkman, and off he went
next door to Mrs. Tubby Bear's house.

Noddy dressed himself in a hurry. "I shall
make a lot of money today," he thought. "People
don't like walking in the rain, especially those
with tails, like Miss Fluffy Cat, or Mr. Monkey.
They get them so wet."

He cleaned his teeth and washed himself. Then
he cleaned his teeth again.

"I forgot to clean you last night, teeth," he said.

9

"That's why I'm cleaning you twice this morning. Now, where's my hair-brush? Hair-brush, where are you? Oh yes, I remember, I put you inside my hat. Did you have a nice cosy night there? Now for my breakfast."

Noddy got out his little car after breakfast and had a good look at it. "You're dirty," he said. "Very dirty. The rain will wash you clean. Good gracious me, I shall get very wet today. I really ought to buy myself a mac."

He was just driving his little car out of the gate when somebody came down the road on a bicycle, ringing his bell loudly. Ting-a-ling-a-ling!

"Big-Ears! Have you come to see me?" called

Noddy, very pleased to see his friend. "I'm just going out to get some passengers in my car. I shall get a lot today because it's so rainy."

"Yes, I know. I've come to lend you my old mac," said Big-Ears, getting off his bicycle. "I've got a new one, see? And I thought of you out in the rain today, so I've come to lend you my old one."

"It will be much too big," said little Noddy. "Oh, Big-Ears, what a most bee-yoot-iful new mac you've got, with a belt and all. I'd like one like that."

"Well, you work hard today and you'll be able to buy one," said Big-Ears. "Get out of the car and put this old mac of mine on. Come along now, no fussing! It doesn't matter if it's too big, it will keep you dry."

Little Noddy had to do as he was told when Big-Ears spoke in such a firm voice, so he got out of his car and put on Big-Ears' old mac. It came right down to his feet! He does look rather peculiar in the picture, doesn't he?

"Turn back the cuffs," said Big-Ears, "then you can drive all right. And don't look so cross. You should smile at me and say thank you, not frown like that."

"Thank you, Big-Ears," said Noddy. "But I don't really like your old mac. Everyone will laugh at me."

Big-Ears went off in a huff, looking enormous in his grand new mac. Noddy drove off to look for passengers. Parp-parp! Who would be the first?

A LITTLE ACCIDENT

"HEY!" called somebody, as Noddy drove round the corner. "Stop, Noddy! I want to hire your car to take me to the market."

It was Mr. Wobbly-Man. Noddy got out to help him into the car, because Mr. Wobbly-Man had no feet.

"It's no fun for me on a rainy day," said Mr. Wobbly-Man. "I wobble into all the puddles and get all splashed and muddy. What's that peculiar thing you've got on, Noddy? Is it an old dressing-gown?"

"No. It's Big-Ears' mac," said Noddy. "I don't like it. The cuffs keep coming over my hands so that I can't steer properly. Ooooh—what a wobble the car gave then—I'll be on the pavement next time if I'm not careful!"

"How rainy it is," said the Wobbly-Man. "Noddy, that mac is so big that you could really let me share half of it. Stop and see if it will go round us both."

Noddy stopped and soon the old mac was round both him and the Wobbly-Man. "Ah—that's better," he said. "I'll pay you double-fare, Noddy. This is fine."

But it was very difficult to drive when somebody else was wearing the same mac, and suddenly Noddy's car swerved again—and knocked down a lamp-post.

"Oh dear—now we've *both* got to get out and put up that lamp-post again," said Noddy, "because we're wearing the same mac. Wait a minute—there's Sally Skittle. I'll ask her to put up the lamp-post for me."

He leaned out of his car. "Sally Skittle! Please could you stand up that lamp-post for me?"

Sally Skittle kindly stood it up—and, will you believe it, Noddy's car knocked it over again as soon as it started off! Bang! Down it went.

And then Mr. Plod came up, frowning. "*I* saw you knock that lamp-post down as soon as kind Mrs. Skittle stood it up, little Noddy. I shall charge you sixpence for making yourself a nuisance. Bring me the money tonight."

"I didn't *mean* to knock it down," said poor
Noddy. "I didn't, I didn't, I didn't, I di . . ."

"I shall charge you a penny for each 'didn't'
if you're not careful," said Mr. Plod, crossly.

"Get on, little Noddy," said the Wobbly-Man.
"It's no use arguing with policemen. I want to
get to the market."

They were soon at the market. Most of the
stalls had umbrellas over them, very gay ones,
striped and coloured. Noddy wished he had one
for his car!

It was quite a difficult job to get Mr. Wobbly-
Man out of Big-Ears' mac. He paid Noddy
double-fare, and wobbled away to do his shopping.
Noddy pulled the big mac round him again. Oh
dear, he felt quite lost in it.

Mrs. Minnie Monkey hurried up to him. "Oh, Noddy! Please will you drive me home. I'm getting my feet so wet!"

She got in and took hold of her tail so that it wouldn't hang from the car. "Do you mind if I put it on your knee, Noddy?" she said. "I've no room on mine because of my shopping basket."

She swung her tail up on his knee. Noddy didn't like it at all. He put it back beside Mrs. Monkey. "It's a very *wet* tail," he said. "It drips down the opening of my mac and wets my legs. Carry your own tail, Mrs. Minnie, please."

MRS. MONKEY SWUNG HER TAIL UP ON NODDY'S KNEE

18

But in half a minute the tail was on his knees again, drip-dripping all over him. Noddy was cross. He took it in his left hand and stuffed it firmly into Mrs. Monkey's shopping-basket. She whisked it out angrily.

"Don't do that! Wetting my cakes and my sugar! Let me stuff it into your mac pocket. It's big enough."

"No," said Noddy and pushed the wet tail away. "I tell you, I don't like your tail, Mrs. Minnie."

The car wobbled when he took his hand from the wheel and crashed into a little red post-box standing at the side of the road. Over it went and began to roll away, all the letters spilling out of it.

"Look at that now!" said Noddy, crossly. "All your fault, Mrs. Minnie. Please get out and put the post-box up again and post the letters in it."

"Certainly not," said Mrs. Monkey. "My goodness, it's rolling down the hill—look! You'd better catch it, Noddy!"

Well, Noddy *had* to get out of the car then, his big mac almost tripping him up. He ran after the red post-box that was now rolling quite fast down the hill. Everyone was jumping out of the way.

Bump! It knocked into someone and down he went. Oh goodness gracious, it was Mr. Plod the policeman! There he was in the road, trying to push the red post-box off himself.

"Who did this?" he roared angrily. Little Gilbert Golly pointed his finger at Noddy.

"*He* did! He rolled it all the way down the hill and knocked you over with it, Mr. Plod! He did!"

"Ooooh, I didn't," said Noddy. "I didn't, I didn't, I di . . ."

"Oh—it's *you* again, is it?" said Mr. Plod in such a stern voice that Noddy left the post-box where it was and scuttled back to his car in fright.

"You come back!" shouted Mr. Plod. "I shall fine you one shilling for knocking me over with the post-box, and one shilling for emptying out the letters and——"

But Noddy didn't wait to hear any more. He drove off at top speed and never even noticed that he was sitting on Mrs. Monkey's wet tail. She was very annoyed.

"Will you get off my tail, Noddy? Noddy, STOP! You're sitting on my TAIL!"

Noddy stopped when he was safely round a corner. He glared at poor Mrs. Minnie Monkey. "I will NOT have that tail of yours in my car any more," he said. "Take it out of my car."

"Very well, I will," said Mrs. Monkey, and got out with her shopping. "If my tail goes, I go too—and we shall *not* pay you a penny, Noddy. In fact I shall complain to Mr. Plod."

"No. Don't do that!" called Noddy in alarm. But Mrs. Monkey had gone off in a temper.

"Oh dear—this isn't my lucky day!" said little Noddy, and on he drove again.

3
EVERYTHING'S GOING WRONG

SOON Mrs. Golly hailed him. "Noddy! Take me to the cake-shop. I've got to meet my sister there and I really can't walk all through these puddles."

Mrs. Golly got into the car. She had an umbrella with her and held it over her head and Noddy's.

"I don't think I want to go right to the cake-shop," said Noddy. "It's opposite the police-station and Mr. Plod is very cross with me this morning."

"Don't be silly. You're a taxi-driver, aren't you?" said Mrs. Golly. "Well, you have to go where your passengers tell you to go. Drive to the cake-shop."

Noddy drove off carefully. Mrs. Golly saw someone she knew across the road and waved her umbrella at her friend.

"Don't do that," said Noddy. "Your umbrella nearly went into my eye. You can't wave umbrellas about in cars."

"Keep your eye out of the way then," said Mrs. Golly. "Oh dear—it's raining harder than ever." She put the umbrella right in front of her face—and Noddy's too—to stop the rain from wetting her hat.

Noddy couldn't see at all, of course. He stopped the car at once and glared at Mrs. Golly. "How can I see through an umbrella?" he said. "Take it away from my face."

"How fussy you are this morning, Noddy," said Mrs. Golly, surprised. "Not a bit like yourself. I'll put the umbrella down if you feel like that and get wet!"

Noddy drove on while Mrs. Golly tried to put the umbrella down. Just as they came to the cake-shop the umbrella was caught by the wind and pulled out of Mrs. Golly's hands—whoooosh!

Noddy was so surprised that he ran straight into a fruit-barrow just in front of him.

Crash! Bang!

NODDY WAS SO SURPRISED THAT HE RAN STRAIGHT INTO A FRUIT-
BARROW JUST IN FRONT OF HIM!

Over went the cart, and apples and oranges rolled about all over the place. "Oh!" squealed Mrs. Golly, and "Hey!" shouted Mr. Tom Teddy, whose barrow it was.

Noddy was just getting out of the car to help to pick up the oranges and apples when he saw the door of the police-station opposite opening —and out came Mr. Plod to see what the crash was.

Poor little Noddy! He got back into his car very quickly indeed. "I didn't, I didn't, I didn't MEAN to!" he shouted to Mr. Plod.

EVERYTHING'S GOING WRONG

Oh dear—now Mrs. Golly was telling Mr. Plod how she had lost her umbrella, and Mr. Tom Teddy was complaining bitterly.

Noddy began to sing very sadly indeed.

> "What an unlucky day,
> Everything's going wrong!
> I think I will run away,
> So, little car, hurry along!
> Nobody likes me at all,
> Everyone's cross as can be,
> I feel very little and small,
> I really am sorry for Me,
> I—really—am—sorry—for—ME!"

4

THE PUDDLY STREET

NODDY soon found himself in a very puddly road indeed. "I'll cheer us up, little car," he said. "We'll drive into all the Very Biggest Puddles, and make great Big Splashes."

So he and the car had a wonderful time in that puddly road. "Here's a fine big puddle!" said little Noddy, driving straight at it. "Whoooosh! In we go!"

My goodness me—what a splash they made!

"That was like a fountain," said Noddy, feeling much better. "Here's another big puddle, car— in we go!"

And in they went at top speed. Splash!

"That puddle was almost like a little pond," said Noddy. "Could you do a *bigger* splash still, do you think? Perhaps you could if you did a little *jump*, car!"

The car was enjoying itself as much as Noddy was. It ran at the next puddle at top speed and gave a jump in the air. WHOOOOOSH! Down it went into the muddy puddle—and there it stayed! It was stuck. It couldn't get out.

And then came the sound of angry voices from two people on the nearby pavement. Noddy turned and saw Mr. and Mrs. Jumbo, covered with mud and water.

"Look what you've made your car do to us!" cried Mr. Jumbo, shaking himself so that drops of water flew everywhere. "We were just walking along quietly, trying not to get into any puddles—when along you come with your car, and splash, you jump into the very biggest puddle, and here we are, covered with mud from head to foot."

"I'm sorry, I'm sorry, I'm sorry," said little Noddy, trying to make his car get out of the puddle. "I didn't mean to, I didn't, I didn't, I didn't, I——"

And of course, just at that very moment, who should come walking round the corner but Mr. Plod! Noddy gave a yell, leapt out of his car and ran away.

"I didn't, I didn't, I didn't!" Mr. Plod heard again, as Noddy ran off down the street, holding up the sides of his much-too-big mac so that he wasn't tripped up.

"What didn't he do this time, Mr. Jumbo?" asked Mr. Plod, surprised. "Really, what is happening to little Noddy today? I'm always coming across him doing something naughty."

"Just look at us—wet from head to foot," said Mrs. Jumbo. "I've got on my new hat too. That little Noddy wants a good spanking, Mr. Plod. That's what he wants."

Mr. Plod took out his notebook and wrote in

" WHAT DIDN'T HE DO THIS TIME, MR. JUMBO ? " ASKED MR. PLOD,
SURPRISED

31

it in his best hand-writing: "One good spanking for Noddy."

"Right," he said. "I'll remember that. Now I'll get his car and take it to the police-station —and there it can stay till Noddy comes back again to fetch it. I'll be waiting with the spanking."

But the little car didn't want to go with Mr. Plod. It hooted loudly and suddenly shot forward out of the mud. Parp-parp! Where was it going to?

It was going to find Big-Ears to tell him to go and look for little Noddy. Noddy had run away! Where, oh where was little Noddy?

So he pushed his blue hat into his pocket and went on his way again. He looked really very peculiar, with Big-Ears' mac down to his heels, and the cuffs hiding his little wooden hands. Noddy turned up the big collar.

"I don't like the rain trickling down my neck," he said. "I washed my neck well last night. Raindrops—you don't need to do it all over again!"

The funny little figure went on and on all alone, down this road and that. Pad—pad—pad. Where are you going, little Noddy. Where are you going?

EVERYONE IS WORRIED

NODDY'S little car drove itself to Big-Ears' toadstool house and stood outside, hooting loudly. Parp-parp.

Big-Ears was baking cakes. He shut the oven door and ran into the garden. "Noddy, is it you?"

But it wasn't Noddy. Only the car stood there giving tiny little hoots as if it wanted to say something important and couldn't.

"Take me to Noddy," said Big-Ears, jumping into the car and taking hold of the steering-wheel. But the car stayed still. It didn't know where Noddy was. "Well, take me to Noddy's house then," said Big-Ears, impatiently, and at once the little car started off and didn't stop till it came to Noddy's dear little House-for-One.

But nobody was there. Mrs. Tubby Bear looked over the wall. "Are you looking for Noddy?" she said. "I'm afraid he has run away. I met Mr. and Mrs. Jumbo out this afternoon and they told me a lot of things about him."

"What did they tell you?" asked Big-Ears, looking very worried.

"Well, he wasn't very well-behaved today," said Mrs. Tubby Bear. "He knocked down a lamp-post and he knocked over a red post-box, and he upset Mr. Tom Teddy's barrow—and then he drove his car through a lot of big puddles and splashed Mr. and Mrs. Jumbo from head to foot."

"Good gracious me!" said Big-Ears, most surprised. "Whatever can have come over him? Do you suppose it was all his fault? He doesn't *usually* go about knocking so many things over."

"I think it must have been something to do with the rain," said Mrs. Tubby. "And, of course, as Mr. Plod was after him, as cross as could be, he got frightened."

"I'll stay in his house tonight and hope he comes back," said Big-Ears. "He's naughty sometimes, but he's very very good at heart, Mrs. Tubby."

"Oh, I know that," said Mrs. Tubby. "We can't do without our dear little Noddy. I'm sure he didn't *mean* to do all those naughty things."

Well, Big-Ears stayed in Noddy's little house

 all night long, but Noddy didn't come back. Big-Ears hardly slept at all, he was so very worried. In the morning he went to Mr. Plod and told him that Noddy had quite gone.

WELL, BIG-EARS STAYED IN NODDY'S LITTLE HOUSE ALL NIGHT
LONG, BUT NODDY DIDN'T COME BACK

Then Mr. Plod was worried. "Oh dear—I hope I didn't frighten him *too* much," he said. "He *was* tiresome yesterday, but I've found out since that Mrs. Monkey was tiresome too, about her wet tail—and Mrs. Golly was quite a nuisance with her umbrella in his car. I expect they upset little Noddy and made him drive into things."

"What are we to do?" asked Big-Ears. "We really must get him back. I shall miss him dreadfully. Toyland won't be the same without him."

"Well, there are only four roads he can take out of this village," said Mr. Plod. "I will send out notices offering a reward to anyone who can say which one Noddy took. Someone will be sure to have noticed him."

So Mr. Plod sent out notices everywhere. They all said the same thing.

LOST. LITTLE NODDY
DRESSED IN BLUE HAT WITH BELL, RED
SHIRT, BLUE SHORTS AND RED SHOES
WITH BLUE LACES. YELLOW SCARF. A
REWARD WILL BE GIVEN FOR ANY NEWS.

But, will you believe it, nobody came with any news at all. Big-Ears looked gloomier than ever, and everyone in Toyland village was worried as could be.

"We've driven him away because we were un-kind to him," said Mrs. Monkey, wiping her eyes.

"I didn't mean to be cross with him," said Mrs. Golly, sniffing.

"Nor did we," said Mr. and Mrs. Jumbo. "Oh dear—we really DO miss little Noddy. Why don't we hear any news of him? Surely plenty of people must have seen him as he ran away?"

41

7

CLOCKWORK CAR TOWN

WELL, of course, plenty of people *had* seen him—but they didn't come and say so because they hadn't known it was Noddy that they met. Big-Ears and Mr. Plod had forgotten that Noddy was wearing Big-Ears' old mac, and that his ordinary clothes couldn't be seen!

"We only met a funny little old man in a coat down to his ankles and his bare head buried deep in a turned-up coat-collar," said everyone. "We didn't see little Noddy in his blue, jingly hat and gay clothes."

What was Noddy doing? Well, you'll never guess! He had gone on and on walking all through the night—and when day came he found himself in Clockwork Car Town.

Noddy was most surprised to see so many cars whizzing by him. One stopped near him and the driver called to him.

"Hey, little fellow! Wind up my car for me, will you? The clockwork has run down."

Noddy went up eagerly and turned the key until he could turn it no more. The driver liked the look of this little fellow in his blue hat and gay clothes, and gave him sixpence.

"Thank you!" said Noddy, picked up Big-Ears' old mac from the ground where he had put it for the moment, and went on his way.

He thought the little clockwork cars were lovely, but he did miss his own car. "Mine's better than these—it doesn't have to be wound up,"

thought Noddy. "Ah—here's another one run down. Sir, shall I wind up your car?"

"Thanks," said the man. "I'm going in for the Great Car Race this afternoon. Are you going to watch it?"

"I don't know anything about it," said Noddy. "But I'd love to go."

"Meet me there, then," said the driver. "I am going in for the race—that is, if I don't feel too upset and nervous! Aren't *you* going in for the race?"

"No," said Noddy. "I haven't got my car with me, or I'd love to. I'll meet you there, sir."

"SIR, SHALL I WIND UP YOUR CAR?"

Well, Noddy wound up a lot more cars and earned quite a bit of money. Then he went to see the Great Car Race, and met the driver he had seen that morning.

Oh dear—he was shaking all over! "I'm all nervous again," he said to Noddy. "I shall never be able to hold the wheel. Will you drive my car in the race for me? I'll share half the prize-money with you if you win."

"Ooooh—can I *really* go in for the race?" said Noddy, in delight. "In this lovely little car of yours? Right—I'll wind it up very very carefully. I'm used to driving my own car—you just watch us go, sir!"

8

THE GREAT CAR RACE

ALL kinds of little clockwork cars began to line up for the race. Noddy's hat jingled loudly, he was so excited, and his head nodded up and down madly. "I do so wish Big-Ears could see me now!" he thought.

Bang! That was the starting signal. Off went the cars at top speed. R-r-r-r-r-r! R-r-r-r-r-r!

Noddy was fourth—then he crept up to third place—then to second! Now he was side by side with a fine big clockwork car driven by a sailor doll. How all the watching toys shouted

in excitement as the cars raced round and round the great ring.

"Faster, faster!" yelled everyone. "This is the last time round!"

Noddy yelled too, and his bell jingled loudly. "Quick, little car, quick!" he cried—and hurrah! the car shot ahead and came in first, its clock-work *just* running down as it went past the winning post!

What an excitement there was! Everyone crowded round little Noddy and clapped him on the back till he almost choked. "Who are you? What's your name?" they cried.

The owner of the car that Noddy had driven came striding up. He gave Noddy an enormous hug.

"You did it! You made my little car win the race! Well done, well done! Here's half the winning money for you!" And he poured so much money on to Noddy's lap that he could hardly believe his eyes! "Oh no!" said Noddy. "Not all this!"

"Yes! I promised you half, you wonderful little fellow!" said the owner and patted Noddy and then patted the little car on its bonnet, too. "My word—I didn't know that my car could go so fast!"

Noddy was very pleased and very excited. He put the money into his pockets and how he clinked and jingled when he walked off! "I'll buy a present for Big-Ears," he thought. "I ll go back home now, because I've got enough money to pay Mrs. Golly for her lost umbrella, and to get a present for Mrs. Monkey because she was upset about her tail."

49

He went on, jingling his money. "And I'll pay Mr. Plod a lot because I knocked over a lamp-post and a post-box, and I'll pay Mr. Tom Teddy for upsetting his cart. Oh yes—and I'll pay Mr. and Mrs. Jumbo for splashing their lovely clothes!"

After he had bought three big ice-creams for

himself, he set off back to his own village again. It would have taken him a long time, but a little wooden engine that came trundling down the road gave him a lift.

"You needn't drive me," said the engine. "I like going by myself. You can sit just behind my funnel if you like."

So Noddy sat behind the funnel and held on to it. The road was bumpy and Noddy jerked up and down, but he didn't mind. He was going home!

SO NODDY SAT BEHIND THE FUNNEL AND HELD ON TO IT

51

"I hope everyone will forgive me for being so naughty," he thought. "But I really didn't mean to be, I didn't, I didn't, I didn't."

He thought he would go and call at Mr. Plod's first and pay him quite a lot of money. Then perhaps he wouldn't be at all cross with him. So he slipped off the little wooden engine just outside the police-station.

"Goodbye and thank you," he said. He put Big-Ears' old mac over his arm and walked over to the police-station. His bell jingled loudly as he knocked at the door. Blam, blam, blam—jingle, jingle, jingle!

9

HOW WONDERFUL!

NOW inside there were quite a lot of people, because everyone was feeling very very worried about little Noddy running away.

There was Mr. Plod, of course, and Big-Ears and the Tubby Bears and Mr. and Mrs. Jumbo and Mrs. Minnie Monkey and Mrs. Golly, the Wobbly-Man, Mr. Tom Teddy and quite a lot of others.

"We *must* find our little Noddy!" said Mrs. Tubby. "I miss him so next door."

"I'll buy him a nice new mac," said Mr. Jumbo. "Then he won't have to wear that enormous old one of yours, Big-Ears."

"And I'll buy him an umbrella—a big one that he can fix over his car when it rains," said the Wobbly-Man.

"I'll give him some of my oranges and apples," said Mr. Tom Teddy. "But WHERE is he?"

There came a sudden knock at the door. Blam, blam, blam! And then another sound— a sound that everyone knew and loved. Jingle, jingle, jingle!

"It's Noddy!" cried Big-Ears. "COME IN!"

The door opened and Noddy peeped in, scared to see so many people there. Oh dear—Mrs. Golly, Mrs. Monkey, the Jumbos, Mr. Tom Teddy —they had all been so cross with him!

He stood there, his little wooden head nodding in excitement.

"I'm sorry, I'm sorry, I'm sorry!" he said, his voice squeaking in fright. "Don't be cross with me. Don't put me in prison, Mr. Plod. Look, I've got enough money to pay you all for the naughty things I did!"

He put his hands into his pockets and pulled them out full of money. "I'll buy you a lovely present, Big-Ears," he said, "and for you, Mrs. Golly, I'll buy——"

But he didn't say another word because Big-Ears had leapt up and run to him. He put his arms round little Noddy and hugged him like a bear.

"Little Noddy! Where have you been? We've worried such a lot about you!"

"We *are* so glad to see you," said Mrs. Golly.

"Welcome back!" said the Jumbos, and everybody said something nice and crowded round little Noddy to pat him on the back and hug him. Mr. Plod came up too, smiling all over his red face.

Noddy ran to hide in a corner when he saw Mr. Plod coming up. "Save me, Big-Ears!" he said. "Don't let him spank me."

"I only just want to hug you, you silly tiresome little rascal of a Noddy," said Mr. Plod. "Now —where have you been?"

He gave Noddy a hug.

"Dear me—isn't anybody cross with me any more?" said Noddy, in wonder. "Oh, I *am* glad. Well—I went to Clockwork Car Town and I drove in the big Race there—and I won it! That's how I got all this money for you!"

"Good gracious! How *wonderful!*" cried everyone, and all at once Noddy was quite a hero. He beamed all over his little wooden face.

"We must tell EVERYONE this!" said Big-Ears in delight. "We always *knew* you were a good driver, Noddy, but we didn't know you could win races. Let's shout out the news in the market-place, and get everyone to cheer you!"

SO THERE THEY GO, AND LITTLE NODDY IS BEING HELD HIGH
UP ON BIG-EARS' STURDY SHOULDERS

So there they go, and little Noddy is being held high up on Big-Ears' sturdy shoulders. "Here comes Noddy, winner of the Great Car Race in Clockwork Town!" trumpeted Mr. Jumbo, and everyone came running up to hear. "Here's our Noddy back again, covered with Glory!"

And now, who is this coming up too? Parp-parp! PARP-PARP-PARP! It is Noddy's little car. What, Noddy is back again? Noddy has driven *somebody else's* car? No, no, that wouldn't do. He must drive his *own* car! Parp-parp-parp! And, as soon as Noddy saw his own little car, he leapt from Big-Ears' shoulder and jumped into the driving seat. Off he went, hooting loudly, and jingle-jingle went his bell.

What a lovely home-coming! Noddy isn't sad any more. He has plenty of money to spend on

his friends, everybody loves him again and he's
a real hero!

Mind that lamp-post, Noddy—be CAREFUL!
Good gracious me, you made it wobble!

> Oh what an excitement!
> What a grand day!
> Noddy is home again,
> Hip-hip-hooray!
> There he goes driving
> In his little car.
> Home is our Noddy,
> How happy we are!